Bonnybridge Primary School
Wellpark Terrace
Bonnybridge

Polly's Absolutely Worst Birthday Ever

First published in Great Britain in 2001
Bloomsbury Publishing Plc, 38 Soho Square, London, W1D 3HB

ISBN 0 7475 5084 0

Printed in Great Britain by Butler & Tanner Ltd, Frome

10 9 8 7 6 5 4 3 2

Polly's Absolutely Worst Birthday Ever

BLOOMSBURY
CHILDREN'S
BOOKS

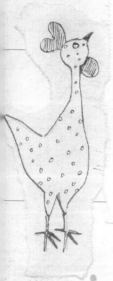

Monday

It is NOT FAIR. I have got the CHICKEN POX and it is my birthday on FRIDAY!!!!

The doctor came round this morning and she said, yes, it is definitely the Chicken Pox and I will have to stay in Quorinteen for a week.

I said, it is not fair because I am feeling better now apart from the spots which are HORRIBLE and itch like mad. She said, yes, but while you have the spots you can give it to someone else. I said, some people deserve spots. It would not

do Darren Biggs any harm
to be itchy for
a bit.

And Alex REALLY deserves them, except that she has already had them, since it was her who gave them to me in the first place.

And then I said to the doctor, but what about my birthday which is on Friday? She said, sorry about that, dear, but can't you have your birthday on another day?

I said, no I can NOT. It is the only ninth birthday I will EVER have.

today

We have to cancel my party!!!!! It was on Saturday!!!!!.

We were going to go to MacDonalds. I had asked Kelly, Alex (huh!), Kate B and Kate M, Freddy and Josh who are boys but quite nice for boys especially Josh, and my cousin Rose.

I don't know why I asked Alex, but she asked me to her party. They had a clown who did tricks. He called her Alex Apple Pie which wasn't very funny, and he called me Polly Pockets which wasn't very funny either.

The tricks were quite good but I had seen most of them at Lauren's party which was YEARS ago. Mummy said Alex's mum had spent a huge amount of money on Alex's party and you would think she had better things to do with her money.

Mummy said, you are really making a bit of a fuss and what about me, I have to stay home all day looking after you. I said, you are home all day anyway because of William. She said, that is not the point.

I am not even allowed to sit in the same room as William in case I give him Chicken Pox. The doctor said that Mopsy will probably catch them anyway. Tee hee.

Mummy said, we will simply have your birthday on another Saturday and that's that. But not next

Saturday because we have people coming for lunch. And not Sunday either because there was something else I can't remember. Anyway it was OBVIOUSLY much more important than my birthday.

She said, poor old Pol, we'll do something nice I promise.

I said, how can it be nice when I will have to spend my birthday at home ITCHING and not being able to see anyone.

When Daddy came home he said, they will put

13

a big red cross on the door
like they did when people
had Plague.

We did Plague in the
Tudors. It was like very
bad Chicken Pox and lots
of people died of it. The
germs came from rats.
They had fleas only they
were worse fleas than you
get on cats. Rose's cat had
fleas this summer but it
did not have Plague. First

14

you sneezed then you got

this ring of big spots then

you went black then you

were dead. The Tudors

had lots of Plague. They
went up and down the
streets with carts and
ringing bells and they said
Bring Out Your Dead and
people put all the dead
bodies on the carts.

I said to Dad, I do not have Plague and no one is coming round saying Bring Out Your Dead.

Dad said, well, not yet, anyway.

Mopsy started to cry and said, I don't want to get the Plague.

I said, you probably won't unless you meet a rat with fleas. But you are going to get the Chicken Pox because the doctor said you will and serves you right.

She cried even more loudly. It was that silly crying she does when she

is just showing off but
Mummy got cross and
said, now, Polly, don't be
unpleasant.

Horace my hamster is
not very well either. He is

not eating his hamster
food.

I counted the spots on
my tummy. There are
seventeen. There are spots
on my back too, only I
can't see them to count.
They are on my face too. I
look horrible. I look like a
pizza.

1

6

13

20

22

28

29

Tuesday

Mum let me phone Kelly. I spoke to Kelly's mum who is NICE. She said, oh, poor Polly, you should have a special treat for being ill on your birthday.

I said, I agree, but no one here seems to think it is anything worth getting worried about when their daughter misses the ONLY ninth birthday she will EVER have.

Kelly's mum said, oh I expect they are worried, poppet.

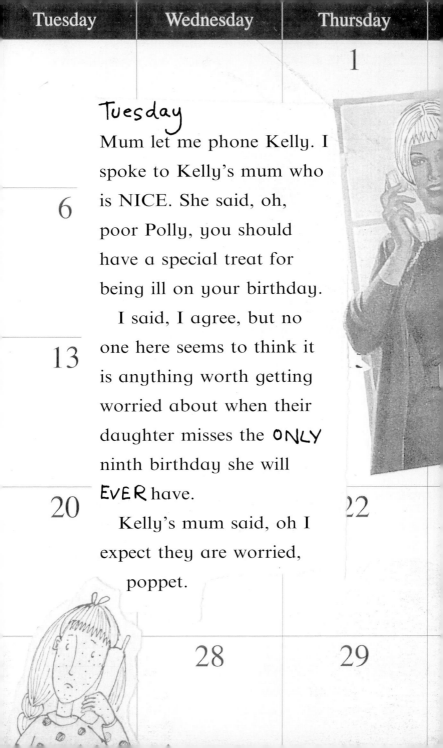

Grown-ups always stand up for each other, even the nice ones.

Then she said, mind I wouldn't mind missing a few birthdays these days. That is another thing about grown-ups, they always pretend they HATE birthdays but they would not be happy if you forgot to send them a card.

Wednesday

Horace is dead!

He just was dead when Mummy got up this morning.

Thursday

I cried all day yesterday.
Well not quite all day but
nearly.

Daddy said, well I'm
sorry, Pol, but for a
hamster Horace was a
very old man – they only
live about two years and
we'd had him for a lot
more than that.

I said, yes, maybe, but
he was still my hamster
and I am sad that he is
dead.

Dad said, yes, I know that, and we'll give him a funeral this evening. Which was yesterday as I did not write anything yesterday because of crying.

This is about Horace dying

Mummy found him. He was just dead in his cage. She said he had died Peacefully in his sleep. I saw him.

He is the only dead thing I have ever seen apart from flies which don't count. He looked just like Horace except he was stiff and pointy and his fur was spiky.

Mopsy wanted to see him. She said, when will he get better? I said he is dead, silly. Dead people don't get better. She said, I know but when will he? I said, he is dead for always and always. She began to cry. I said never mind, he was a very old man for a hamster, and she said no he wasn't he was a little hamster boy. She does not understand things. She is only just four.

When Daddy came home we did the funeral. We put Horace in a little box wrapped up in paper handkerchiefs. I put some flowers in the box.

Then Daddy dug a hole at
the end of the garden
under the tree. We all
stood round. Mopsy cried
but I had stopped crying
by then. Dad said,
goodbye, Horace, old
chap. For a hamster you
were really quite nice and
we are going to miss you.

Mummy said, goodbye, Horace, we very much enjoyed having you as one of the family. We will remember lots of things about you.

William came out in his push-chair but he did not say anything except gaa gaa as he is too young.

Mopsy said, goodbye, Horace poo-face. She can be silly like that.

I said, we are very sorry you are dead, Horace. You were very cute and we always liked you except

when you ran away and
when you bit my thumb
that time. I said, I hope
you forgive Mopsy for
that time she tried to
strangle you, she was only

a baby then. Also it was
not kind of her to put you
in the Fisher Price house
as you did not fit and you
were not a toy as I kept
telling Mopsy only she did
not listen.

Then Daddy said, all
right, Polly, we'll cover
him up now and I'll plant
some daffodil bulbs on top.

Then we went in and had
green pasta with cheese.

Friday

This is the morning of my
absolutely most horrible
birthday EVER.

Mummy said, happy
birthday, darling, here is
your card. I said, it is not
going to be a happy
birthday as Horace is dead
and I have got Chicken Pox.

Mummy said, we will make it as nice as possible and don't you want to see your presents, they are downstairs?

I said I did.

I went downstairs and it was a new Arsenal strip and these Really Good trainers! which I need as my others are getting too small.

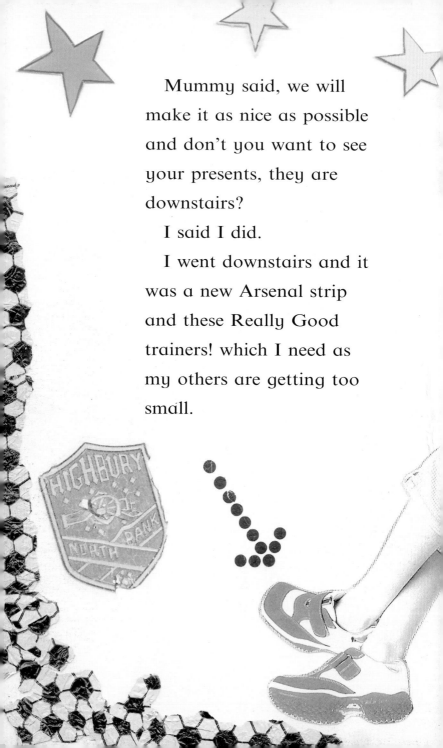

The post came and I
had six cards, one from
Rose who is my nearly-
cousin, one from Kelly,
one from Gran and

Grandad in Scotland, one
from English Granny and
Grandad, one from Uncle
Max in Australia, and one
from Aunt Sammy and
Uncle Phil.

34

Later

Granny phoned and said
could she come over.

She came at three and
said we'd have a proper
old-fashioned birthday
party just like she used to
have when she was a little
girl, Mopsy and me and
Mummy and Granny and
William were there.

Granny had brought fish
paste and cress sandwiches
(yuk – but she said she
liked them when she
was little), jellies in
paper cases with
bits of peach in
and a cake

she had made with pink
icing on. Granny said pink
icing was really just the
same as white icing but
she thought it tasted better
when she was a little girl.

For her present she
bought me a Really Nice
backpack in pink and
green. Normally I do not
like pink but this was
Really Nice.

Happy Birthday To *ME*

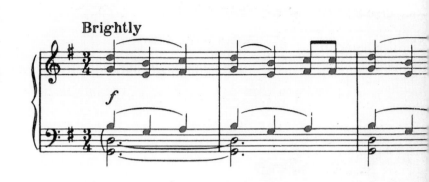

Brightly

f

Hap-py birth-day to you, Hap-py birth-day to you,

mf

G

We sang Happy Birthday. I had to join in as there were not enough people there. I sang Happy Birthday to Me. (Mopsy sang Happy Birthday to Me too, even though it was not her birthday). Then we played old-fashioned games.

From good friends a

G

C

old friends and new, May good luck go with you, And hap

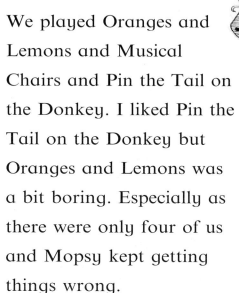

We played Oranges and Lemons and Musical Chairs and Pin the Tail on the Donkey. I liked Pin the Tail on the Donkey but Oranges and Lemons was a bit boring. Especially as there were only four of us and Mopsy kept getting things wrong.

Oranges and Lemons

On the whole I prefer
new-fashioned parties but
it was quite fun.

Then the doorbell went
and it was Kelly. She
could not come in because
of the Quorinteen but she
came to the door. She had
a present for me. She had

42

this HUGE card. Mrs
Shah had written Happy
Birthday Polly and we are
sorry about the Chicken
Pox. She did not know
about Horace or I expect
she would have written
that she was sorry about
Horace too. Everybody in
the class had signed it.

Josh had signed it!
Everyone says Josh is my
boyfriend BUT HE IS
NOT !!!!! I do NOT have a
boyfriend. Josh is quite
nice though, for a boy.

Kate
x

Josh

love Rose
xx

Love from
Alex

Happy Birthday
spotty
Polly

DARREN
BIGGS

HAPPY
Birthday

Darren Biggs had
signed Happy Birthday
Spotty Polly. I hope he
gets Chicken Pox too.

I opened Kelly's
present. It was bubble
bath and strawberry
soap. Mopsy said, she

love from
Kelly x

45

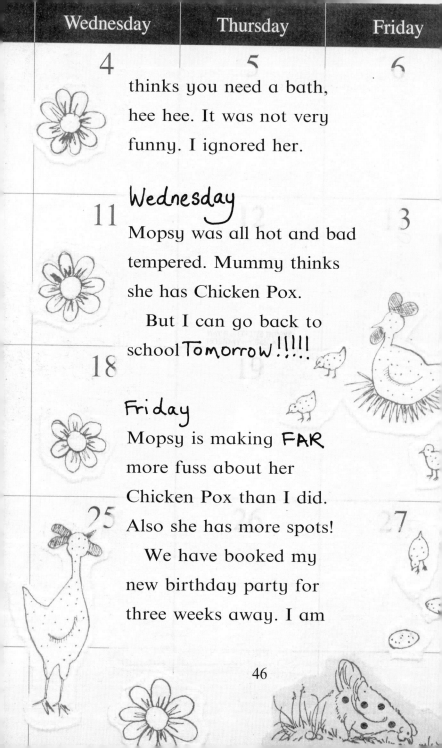

4   5   6

thinks you need a bath,
hee hee. It was not very
funny. I ignored her.

Wednesday

11

Mopsy was all hot and bad
tempered. Mummy thinks
she has Chicken Pox.

But I can go back to
school Tomorrow!!!!!

18

Friday

Mopsy is making FAR
more fuss about her
Chicken Pox than I did.
Also she has more spots!

25

We have booked my
new birthday party for
three weeks away. I am

going to send out the invitations today.

Kelly has Chicken Pox too. It is all Alex's fault.

Saturday

(Not the next Saturday because I could not be bothered to write for a bit. Kelly is back at school now and Mopsy is back at nursery. I think that's all the important things that have happened up till now. But the next thing is REALLY important.)

Mummy and Daddy said, we have been thinking. They said,

perhaps now Horace is dead we ought to have another pet. Though we know there can never be another Horace.

I said, goody can we have a puppy?

BOW WOW

Rubber Puppy

A, part of flowering plant; B, part of lower surface of leaf—upper surface similar; C, part of calyx, inne... ...face; F, keel an... ...um; H

Daddy said, no, we thought about a dog, but it would not be fair. We are out all day and Mummy will be out all day when she goes back to work. We will not be able to look after a dog properly.

T for TIGER

Dogs need lots and lots
of walks so they can do
their poos.

I said, what pet will we
have then?

Mopsy said, I want a
panda I want a baby tiger
I want a koala. She can be
quite silly at times. I said,
shut up, Mopsy they aren't
pets. I said, then can
we have a kitten?

51

Mummy said, that is what we thought.

I went, WHAT, REALLY ????

They went, yes, really.

I went HOORAY HOORAY We're going to have a kitten.

I said, can we get it from Animal Rescue?

Mummy said, Oh you and your Animal Rescue, Polly.

I said, well it's nice to rescue things. Which is true.

They said, well there is an Animal Shelter near somewhere, I forget where, but not far away.

They gave me the talk
about how kittens would
grow up and become cats

and we would have to look
after it all that time and
how they were NOT TOYS
and did not like being
picked up all the time and
dressed up.

I know all this already so
it was really more for
Mopsy than me. Alex used
to dress their cat up and

now it runs away all the time when it sees her.

I said, can I phone Kelly? She cannot have a cat because they give her mum the heebie-jeebies. The heebie-jeebies are what I get when I see brocerly. They said, yes you can, then I thought maybe it wouldn't be nice to phone her to say, we are getting a cat, when she can't have one. I shall tell her on Monday and she can come and visit our cat when we have one.

55

Daddy said, that is very thoughtful, Polly.

Well I am more thoughtful than some people.

Saturday

We are going to the Animal Shelter tomorrow!!!!!

Today we went to the pet shop. We bought some cat litter and a cat tray

(yuk) a basket to bring him
back from the shelter in,

a bowl
and some kitten food.

Also some toys –

a ball on a string
and a mouse.

57

I said to Mopsy, remember these are cat toys not toys for you, and she said, I'm not stupid, der-brain. Mopsy is getting quite bossy these days. Of course, she wanted to get this little collar with diamonds on.

It was gross. Mummy said he won't need a collar yet

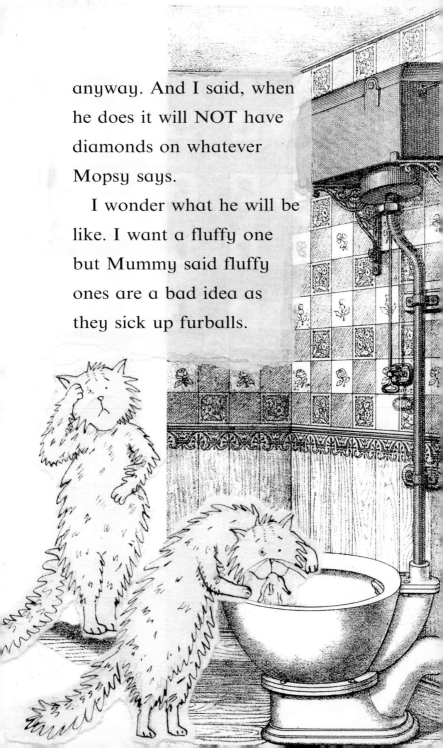

anyway. And I said, when he does it will **NOT** have diamonds on whatever Mopsy says.

I wonder what he will be like. I want a fluffy one but Mummy said fluffy ones are a bad idea as they sick up furballs.

It might be tabby or it might be black and white. I do NOT want a ginger one.

Tomorrow we will have a Kitten !!!!!!!!!!!!!!

kitten

The Toozleum Cat.

Sunday at ten o'clock

We are going to see the lady at the shelter at eleven. She is called Paula. Mummy says she sounds nice on the phone.

I can't write any more now but I will try and put it all in later if I am not too excited!

Later

I am too excited.

More Later

I am still excited but I am not too excited and they are asleep now so I can write about them.

When we got to the shelter Paula was there. She was nice. She said come this way and we went into a room with all these cages. There were lots and lots of cats. Some were ugly and some were

old. Mummy said we were sorry for the old and ugly ones but what we really wanted was a kitten. Paula said she understood.

62

There were two lots of
kittens. One lot were
blotchy and they looked
cross. I hoped we would
not end up with them.
Then Paula took us to this
other cage and there were
two REALLY CUTE kittens.
One was all black and one
had white blotches on its
face. It was blotchy but

not ugly so I did not mind. Paula said they had two brothers who had just found homes. Their mother was in the next cage. She did not seem very interested in them so I suppose she was not a very good mother.

We opened the cage and Paula let us pick them up and take them out. They were much much bigger than Horace. (I have not forgotten about Horace. I will never forget Horace.) They had little whiskers and big eyes.

I said I don't know

which one I like best.
Mopsy said she liked the
blotchy one but she wasn't
sure because she liked the
other. They meowed and
meowed at us. They
Deffinitly wanted to have
us for owners. Paula said,
look they really like you.

Then I said, Mummy
can't we have two of them?
And she said, well . . . in
her changing her mind
voice. I said, go on. She
said well, I ought to phone
Daddy and see. She had
her mobile so she phoned
Daddy. Then she said, he
says all right we can!!!!

Mopsy said Hooray and
I said Hooray and Paula
said hush, you'll frighten
all the cats.

Then we went to the
desk and there was
another lady there. She
was not nice like Paula,
she was very strict. She
asked us all these

questions about did we
have a garden and would
we take them to the vet.

Then she looked at me
and Mopsy and said, you
do realise that cats aren't
toys, and they won't be
kittens for ever and we'll
have to look after them,
and we mustn't keep
picking them up.

I said I knew all that because Alex keeps picking her cat up all the time and now it runs away from her. I said I would make sure that Mopsy didn't keep picking them up and

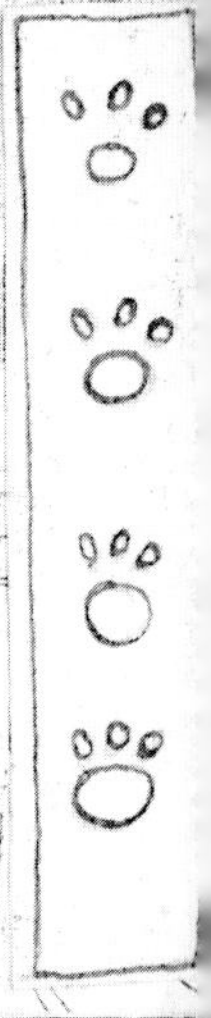

1

A

2

3

4

M

B

when William was bigger I'd make sure he didn't either. She said, oh dear, how many children have you got (to Mummy), and afterwards Mummy said she was afraid that she wasn't going to let us have the kittens after all.

Anyway in the end she let us have them. Which was **Very kind of her I don't think** as I said to Mummy in the car because if we had not rescued them they would have ended up on a rubbish dump or something, so we were being nice. And from the way she went on you would think we were just being **REALLY HORRID**.

We said mine was the black one and Mopsy's was the blotchy one.

In the car they meowed all the way home. They have such little tiny meows. When

we got home we opened
the box and Mopsy's one
went straight behind the
sofa. My one ran around
the room sniffing. I think
my one is much cuter.

We tried to play with
my one but she was too
busy sniffing. She does not
meow, she makes these
funny little squeaks.
Mopsy's one was still
hiding. Then we put some
food out on a piece of
paper on the floor and
Mopsy tried to push food
into my one's mouth. I

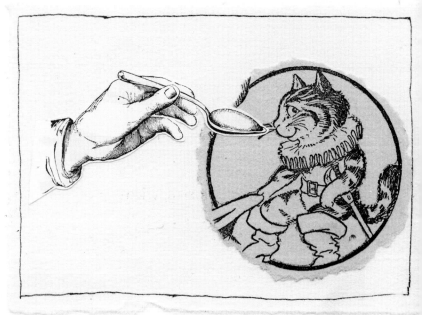

told her off but she would
not listen until Mum told
her off too. Her kitten was
still hiding.

He did come out in the
end.

I forgot to say my one is
a girl and Mopsy's one is
a boy.

I also forgot to say what
their names are but I can't

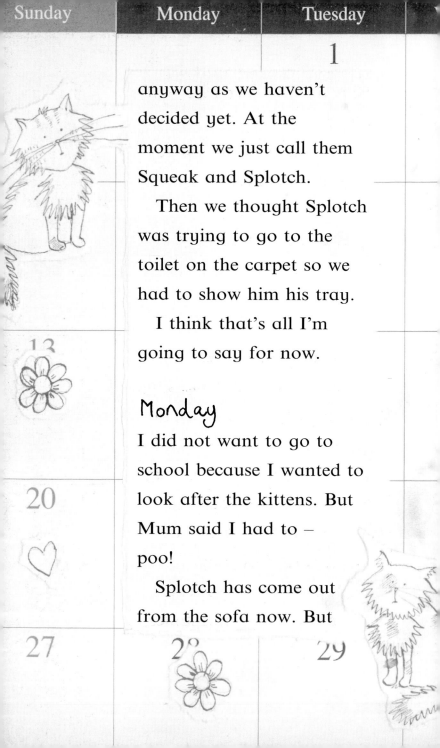

Sunday	Monday	Tuesday
		1

anyway as we haven't decided yet. At the moment we just call them Squeak and Splotch.

Then we thought Splotch was trying to go to the toilet on the carpet so we had to show him his tray.

I think that's all I'm going to say for now.

Monday

I did not want to go to school because I wanted to look after the kittens. But Mum said I had to – poo!

Splotch has come out from the sofa now. But

he is a bit of a scaredy-cat, ha ha.

Mum said, what about Salt and Pepper?

We said, No.

She said, what about Marks and Spencer?

We said No No.

She said, what about French and Saunders?

I said, this is getting silly.

She said, well I'm trying my best.

I said, you can't just say 'something and something' and pretend it's a name.

She said, I give up.

Mopsy said, I want to call my one Melanie Jones.

31

Melanie Jones is her best friend from school. I said you can't:

a because you can't call a cat somebody Jones and

b because Melanie is a girl's name and your one is a boy.

I was so excited about the kittens that I forgot to put another REALLY important thing.

I AM GOING TO HAVE MY BIRTHDAY
ON SATURDAY

I said, promise me I
REALLY REALLY am
going to have my
birthday.

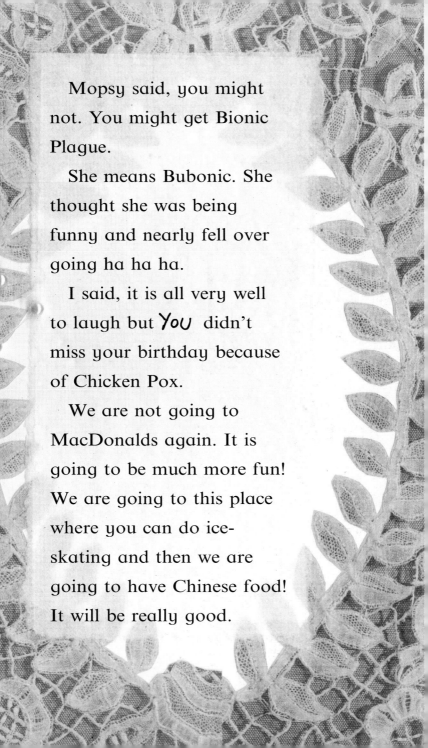

Mopsy said, you might not. You might get Bionic Plague.

She means Bubonic. She thought she was being funny and nearly fell over going ha ha ha.

I said, it is all very well to laugh but YOU didn't miss your birthday because of Chicken Pox.

We are not going to MacDonalds again. It is going to be much more fun! We are going to this place where you can do ice-skating and then we are going to have Chinese food! It will be really good.

I have asked the same people again. Everyone can come except Kate M. which is all right as I am not partickerly keen on her.

Alex said, Josh is coming because he is your boyfriend. You love him.

I said, he is not my boyfriend and I do not love him.

She said, yes and you are going to marry him.

I said, I am NOT going to marry him. I do not have to decide now who I am going to marry.

She went on and on and on.

80

Josh is quite nice. I acksherly like him. But he is NoT NoT NoT my boyfriend.

We still do not have names for the kittens.

Squeak – my one – is very clever. She has found out how to go upstairs. She climbs up and then she walks around looking everywhere and going Mwa mwa in this funny

tiny little squeaky voice. I must
give her proper meowing
lessons.

She does not like playing
with her cat toys but there is
this bit of string she really
loves. And she pretends the rug
is a mouse and tries to kill it.

She is really cute. I wish
she had a name.

Tuesday

Mum said, it's a pity they
aren't both boys because
then they could be Wallace
and Grommit.

Dad said, what about
Wallace and Grommeta?

This was not one of his
best ideas.

Wednesday

Gran sent a list of names:
    Sooty and Sweep (no)
    Popeye and Olivoil (no)
    Marks and Spencer (no
for Mummy and still no)

83

Bubble and Squeak (no to Bubble)

Dot and Carry (Why?)

Romeo and Juliet (*Deffinitly* no)

Jack and Jill (*boRING*)

Topsy and Turvy

I think she should stop.

Thursday

Mrs Shah said, shall we all think of names for Polly's kittens?

Kelly said Little and Large.

Alex said Dinky and Winky. This just shows you the kind of person she is. I will NOT have cats called Dinky and Winky.

Jason said Dracula and
Vampire.

Darren Biggs said Snot
and Bogey. He would.

Kate M said Fluffy and
Furry.

Karen said Brandy and
Whisky.

SPENCER

1

2

MARKS 7

9

Freddy Billings said Marks and Spencer.

There were more but I cannot remember them. Some of them were quite silly.

Josh said, why did we have to have new names. He said he thought Splotch and Squeak were quite good names.

Acksherly, I think he is right.

He can be quite sensible for a boy, sometimes.

21

Friday

Today when Squeak was washing herself I said

28

Squeak to her and she
stopped her washing and
looked up at me. So now I
think it is her name.

Mopsy said Melanie Jones was not her best friend today, her best friend was Jade. She does not know what a best friend is if she thinks you have a new one every day. So I said We are not calling the cat Jade, stupid, and she said, I didn't say we were, stupid, and Mummy said, now now girls and are we decided on Squeak and Splotch because they are quite nice names after all.

It is my party tomorrow! We are going in three cars!!

from

Swings

leaves

5

Granny is coming to look after William, then Mummy will take me and Kelly (good) and Alex (poo) and Josh (good) in her car and Daddy will take Mopsy and Kate and Freddy. Aunt Sammy will come along with Rose because they are the same family. First we are going to the sports centre for skating then we

are off to the Golden
Dragon.

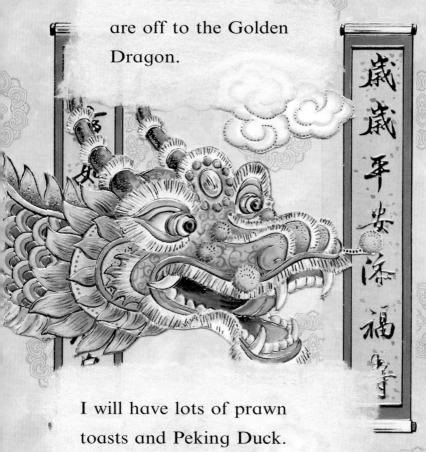

I will have lots of prawn
toasts and Peking Duck.

Sunday
I am so tired today. It was
really good yesterday.

It was so funny, Alex
goes on and on about how
she always does skating
and how brilliant she is.
Then she fell down
THREE TIMES.

It was so funny. I only fell
down once if you don't
count when Kate bumped
into me and I don't
because that was her fault.

Kelly did not fall down
at all. She is really good.

The boys went all silly
OF COURSE. Sometimes I
wonder what boys are for.
Mopsy is a rubbish skater.
Rose had never done it
before so she did fall down
a bit but she was REALLY
good for a first time.

It was so stupid,
everyone went, Josh is
your boyfriend, and I went
no he is NOT.

The Chinese food was really nice.

I got good presents. Kelly gave me a video,

Alex gave me a head band with flowers on,

Kate gave me a quite nice pencil case,

Josh gave me a book,

Freddy gave me a box of fudge

and Rose gave me a really nice T-shirt.

I said to Josh, it is so stupid, everyone says you are my boyfriend, but I do not have a boyfriend. He said it is really stupid. He said his brother has a girlfriend and all they do is keep trying to snog.

I said YUK I was not going to snog him and he said he was not going to snog me.

It was quite late when we got home. I was really tired. Dad said, well, Polly, how do you feel about your birthday now?

I said my birthday was still REALLY HORRIBLE and they were not going to make me forget it EVER. You could not forget Horace dying and being itchy with the Chicken Pox and having to cancel MacDonalds.

He said, I know all that, Polly, but did you enjoy yourself today?

I said, oh yes, it was really, really great.

HAPPY BIRTHDAY!